D0247223

BATTLE
OF THE
CYBORG
CAT

3 8002 02403 735 2

To my mum Christianah and my late father Bola.
They helped nurture my love of books and reading.

www.studiopressbooks.co.uk

Written by Ade Adepitan
Illustrated by David M. Buisán
Designed by Janene Spencer
Edited by Jasmine Richards

A CIP catalogue record for this book is available from the British Library.

Paperback: 978-1-78741-325-2
Printed and bound by Clays Ltd, St Lives Plc
2 4 6 8 10 9 7 5 3

Studio Press is an imprint of Bonnier Publishing company
www.bonnierpublishing.co.uk

ADE ADEPITAN

Hey, how are you doing? My name is Adedoyin Olayiwola Adepitan. I know what you're thinking: That name must be worth a lot of points in a game of *Scrabble!* You'd be right. You may know me off the telly. I'm that guy who uses a wheelchair and is pretty good at basketball. I present quite a few shows, as well.

My family call me Doyin, which is the second part of my first name. My mum calls me by my full name, but only when I'm in trouble. Most of my friends call me Ade – not like the end of the word 'lemon-ade'. And not like the letters 'A', 'D' and DEFINITELY NOT EDDIE! But more like the sound 'a' and the letter 'D'. Try it: A-dee! Got it.

My book, *Ade's Amazing Ade-Ventures,* is set in the 1980s. Okay, yeah, I know that's a long time ago (no need to be cheeky now). The story is based on the time I moved to London with my family and started going to school here. The UK was very different back then; it was a time of interesting music, questionable fashion, severe haircuts (if you don't believe me, have a look at some of your mum and dad's old school pics) and, of course, it was when dad dancing was invented...

Moving home can be very difficult. Moving to a completely different country to start a new life, well that's just scary. Especially when you realise that some people in your new neighbourhood might not like you because you look different to them. On top of all that, I'd had polio as a baby, so I also had to wear a heavy iron brace called a caliper on my left leg, and ugly-looking hospital boots, just so I could walk. Hospital boots: great for putting in a heavy tackle on the football pitch, terrible for dancing and absolutely impossible not to stick out like a sore thumb whenever you're wearing them!

But you know what? The caliper is why my friends started to call me Cyborg Cat. Don't know what a cyborg is? That's okay. Keep reading and you'll find out!

CHAPTER 1

QUEEN'S MARKET

"Oi, why don't you go back to your own country and take the little cripple boy with you?" These were the first words anyone had said to Ade and his parents since they left the airport. *In fact,* Ade thought, not daring to look over his shoulder, *if you ignore the customs officer who only grunted hello, and the police officer who pointed to where the train station was, these are the first words any British person has ever said to us.* Ade swallowed hard, the air here suddenly tasting very different from that back in Nigeria.

"Don't take any notice, Doyin," Dad muttered.

Mum's jaw was tight. "Just keep walking." She glanced over her shoulder. "Quickly. Keep walking. Quickly."

Dad didn't hesitate; he scooped up Ade and put him on his shoulders. Then he picked up the suitcase once more and strode on.

Ade knew he was small for a nine-year-old. *But still*. "Wait! I wanted to walk-" he broke off as he felt his father's grip on him tighten and the metal of his caliper give a little squeak of protest as if also warning him to be quiet. It seemed to be saying, *There's danger nearby, shhh.*

Ade looked down at his mum and saw that she had moved in closer to his dad.

They strode on past a few market stalls, keeping their heads down. Ade caught a glimpse of a sign that read Queen's Market and could hear the call of traders selling everything from fruit, to fish, to trousers that they called Farahs.

The colour, chaos, hustle and bustle of the busy market didn't seem all that different to markets back home in Nigeria. If Ade hadn't heard that mean, angry voice behind him, he'd be thinking how easy it would be in this new country. *But I did hear that voice.*

As Ade and his parents came alongside a stall selling Jif and other bottles promising 'the ultimate shine for your bathroom', a group of men barged past them. Ade counted four in total and they stood in a line to block the way ahead. They all had very short hair and were wearing white T-shirts, braces, jeans and green jackets with Union Jack flags on them.

The shortest one looked the meanest. He stared at them with bloodshot eyes and a smell rolled off him that made Ade's nose sting. It reminded him of how his Uncle Lanre used to smell when he came back from a party. It was so strong that Ade put his finger under his nose.

The short man didn't like that and spat on the floor right by Dad's feet.

"Please," said Ade's father. "We don't want any trouble. We just want to get to our house."

"Yeah, well we don't want you or your type here," shouted one of the other men. "So go back to your house in Bongo Bongo Land."

The men all laughed at that, but it wasn't a funny, happy laugh. To Ade, they sounded like dogs being strangled. *Where is this Bongo Bongo Land?* he wondered. Had his parents bought a house there without telling him? *They should have discussed it with me. I'll be 10 next year.*

"And we don't want stupid cripples here, either," said the man at the front.

Stupid cripple? Ade tried to get his head around that. *I wear a caliper that supports my leg but that doesn't make me a cripple and it doesn't make me stupid.*

Ade was scared but he also had to know why this man, who had never met him before, thought he was stupid.

His mum was quicker. She stepped forwards and looked right into the man's bloodshot eyes and shouted, "He's not a stupid cripple!"

Mum's back was as straight as a ruler and she was so angry she was shaking. Back home, when Mum got angry people were scared of her, but that wasn't happening with these men. They just seemed to think it was very funny and started laughing that horrible laugh again.

The market around them had fallen silent. There was no more hustle and bustle. The other market traders and shoppers were all looking over in their direction. All those eyes watching them made Ade feel like they were on display or something.

Looking around, Ade's gaze met with one of the traders, a big man wearing a funny-looking checked hat. He looked upset. *Then help us,* Ade thought. His heart was beating so fast he thought it might burst out of his chest.

The trader took a step forwards, but one of the men, the tallest one, screwed up his face and pointed a finger towards the guy's face. "Don't even think about it!" he snarled.

The trader and everybody around him quickly looked away and carried on as if nothing had happened. Ade didn't think it was possible, but his heart started to beat even faster.

The four men laughed again, but a moment later they stopped and the one at the front with the smelly breath looked at Ade's father, his eyes full of hatred and menace.

"Right," he said. "I'm going to give you five seconds to turn round and get out of here." He patted his jacket pocket. "Or else."

"**One.**"

"**Two.**"

"Come on." Mum's voice trembled. "We'll find another way."

"**Three.**"

Mum tugged on Dad's arm. "Come on."

"**Four.**"

Ade's father stared at the man, refusing to look away. "We're going," he said. Then they turned round and walked out of the market the way they'd come, the sound of the men's laughter ringing in their ears.

CHAPTER 2

NOT A GREAT BREAKFAST

There's never a good time to be given bad news, but nine o'clock in the morning, when you're hungrily shovelling a large spoonful of Sugar Puffs and warm milk into your mouth, is definitely one of the worst times.

"Oh, by the way, Doyin, we're going to have a party tomorrow to celebrate our arrival in England. It's been a few weeks now and we have a lot to give thanks for."

Unfortunately for Ade, he'd already put the cereal in his mouth so, "Mmmm, whhuuummmm dufff dooossshhhaaa," was the only response he could manage.

"Oh good, I know how much you like a party," Mum said. "I've invited all your cousins, aunties and uncles, and our family friends as well." She smiled. "We can all get dressed up."

"No! No, we can't," Ade said in a spray of Sugar Puffs. He imagined himself in a pair of loose-fitting trousers and an oversized but ornate-looking shirt. "People don't wear sokoto and agbada here."

His mum frowned. "Ade, it's a party. Our party. We need to look good. Anyway, I've already picked your outfit."

Ade groaned inwardly. Nigerian traditional dress came in all sorts of patterns and he knew his mum wasn't interested in the bland, boring styles. She had what you could call a very interesting dress sense, though another way of describing it might be an outrageous, completely over the top, what on earth is she thinking, dress sense. She always chose the brightest and loudest colours for Ade to wear.

"Okay, fine," Ade sighed. "I guess it's just family anyway. I'll stay inside."

Mum waved a hand. "Well yes, them and those young boys we saw playing football on our street last week."

Ade felt the spoon slip from his fingers. It clattered to the floor. "Mum! Why did you do that? We don't even know them!"

"Doyin." Mum was chuckling and Ade could tell that she thought he was over-reacting. "It's important for you to make new friends. You love playing football and so do they. Everything's going to be fine."

"It's not going to be fine!" Ade shouted, his cheeks getting hot and his eyes stinging with tears. "They're going to think I'm weird and laugh at me."

Before his mum could say anything else, he hopped down from the table, thudded up to his room and slammed the door shut.

Ade threw himself on his bed, his face buried in his pillow. His mum didn't get it. After what happened in Queen's Market, Ade had decided that the best thing he could do was to keep as quiet as possible and not draw any attention to himself. *If no one can see you or hear you, then they can't be nasty to you,* he'd decided. *I'll just stay in my room, with my action figures and* X-Men *comics all summer. And if I do have to leave the house I'll wear a hat and make sure my caliper is covered up.*

Ade's plan was working well so far. Since that day in the market there hadn't been any more problems with nasty, smelly men, but parties were big and noisy and full of people, which was exactly the sort of thing that would draw attention to Ade and his family. And Nigerian parties were the biggest and the noisiest of them all.

Ade heard footsteps on the stairs and quickly dived under his covers.

"Hmm, I wonder where Doyin could be?" Mum said as the door clicked open.

Ade said nothing and lay as still as he could.

"Oh well," Mum went on, "I'll just have to sit on the end of the bed. Sit RIGHT HERE and wait till he comes back."

What? Ade didn't fancy getting squished beneath her bottom and so swiftly crawled up through the blankets and emerged into the daylight.

"Oh, there you are, Doyin." Mum sat down next to him and gave him a hug.

In return, Ade snivelled and felt a little embarrassed because his tears had taken even him by surprise.

His mother gently kissed his forehead and said softly, "Don't cry Doyin, why would those boys laugh at you?"

"Maybe because of my caliper?" *And because it makes me look like C3PO from* Star Wars *but with chewing gum stuck to the bottom of my left foot.*

She shook her head. "When they see how talented, intelligent and handsome you are they will love you, not laugh at you."

She pinched his cheeks and stared down at him with her big bright eyes. She had a way of making him feel better with one look, but he still didn't believe her.

CHAPTER 3

PLANS A, B, C AND D

It was the day of the party and his mum had been cooking all morning. She'd even sent Dad out for more food. Sniffing the air, Ade could tell she was cooking all his favourite dishes: fried plantain, chicken and his much-loved moi moi - a steamed bean pudding that had no business tasting as good as it did considering it was made of beans! That much food meant an awful lot of people.

Including the boys from my street, Ade reminded himself. He rested his head against the kitchen table. *This is going to be a disaster.*

"Oh Doyin, don't look so sad." Ade's father staggered into the kitchen and put down the heavy shopping. "Do you want some jelly?"

Before Ade had a chance to react, Dad swept him up into the air.

"No Dad, not the jelly hands," Ade squealed. But it was too late. Dad made his hands go all wobbly like jelly and tickled him. Ade couldn't help but laugh until tears ran down his cheeks, but afterwards, when they were both tired and lying on the floor, Ade started thinking about the party again and he felt knots tightening in his stomach.

Then Dad went and made things even worse. "I can't wait for the party to start." He jumped to his feet. "I'm going to show everyone my best dance moves!"

Ade looked at Mum. They both knew what was coming next.

"Oh yeah, who's the daddy?!" Dad said as he moved to the centre of the room. He started making weird high-pitched noises, stamping his feet and flailing his arms about wildly in what he probably thought were some of his best dance moves, but, by anyone else's standards, would probably have been their worst.

As he gyrated, he clattered into some pots and pans. Then he bumped into a chair and fell on it. Almost in one motion, whilst landing on the chair, he placed his right leg over his left and sat upright with folded arms. He gave Ade and Mum a knowing look, like falling in the chair was part of the move. He nearly pulled it off, as well, until a saucepan that had been resting precariously on the shelf behind

him wobbled and fell off. It landed on the top of Dad's neatly combed Afro with a ***BONG.***

Ade covered his face with his hands. *There's only one thing for it,* he thought. *I have to get this party cancelled.*

* * *

"I see, sir, so you would like one hundred mice delivered to your house this afternoon?"

Ade was on the phone to the local pet shop, Petty Minded. He'd found their number in something called *The Phone Book*, which was basically the biggest book in the world full of page after page after page of phone numbers. Ade couldn't understand why anyone would want to read a book like that, but on page 1437 he'd found the number and dialled it.

The idea was simple: scatter the mice all over the house. Mum and Dad would think that all the food they'd been cooking had attracted them and they were now overrun with the creatures. No one would want to come to a house infested with mice, so they'd definitely have to cancel the party.

Ade had put on the deepest voice he could to speak to the man in the shop and so far it seemed to be working.

"Yes, that's right," he said.

"Very good," said the man. "Could I take an address for the delivery, please?"

"I live at 4 Parsons Road in Plaistow," Ade said proudly. His parents had made him learn the address off by heart almost as soon as they'd moved in, just in case he ever got lost and had to tell someone where he lived.

"Thank you, sir," said the man. "So that's one hundred mice, plus delivery charge. That will be forty pounds exactly. Will that be cash or cheque?"

Uh-oh, Ade thought as he realised the major flaw in his otherwise perfect plan. *I have no money.*

"Erm, I, erm, I've changed my mind," he

said quickly. "And I need to go to the toilet. Bye."

Nice work. Ade shook his head. *Especially the toilet detail. Nope, I don't think I'll be visiting Petty Minded any time soon. Or ever, for that matter.*

* * *

Luckily, Ade's second plan was much simpler and, most importantly, didn't involve him having to phone anyone or spend money.

You can't have a party without music, Ade mused. *All I have to do is get rid of all my parents' records.* He nodded to himself. *Easy-peasy. Just don't get caught. I'll be like a cat burglar trying to steal the Crown Jewels.*

Very quietly and very slowly, he crept downstairs and into the front room. He could hear Mum and Dad in the kitchen, chatting and joking, which was actually very helpful. His dad had a really loud voice, so they were even less likely to hear him.

Ade stopped in front of his parents' record collection. There seemed to be a lot more records than he remembered. He'd planned to take them up to his room, one by one, and hide them under the bed, but the party would be over before he'd removed half of them.

Ade shrugged, grabbed a bunch and sneaked out of the room as quietly as he could. He was halfway up the stairs, when three of the records escaped from their sleeves and made a run for it.

Two of the records flopped down a couple of steps and stopped. The third record had other ideas. Big ideas. It bounced down all the steps like a spinning wheel then carried on along the corridor.

"Come back," whispered Ade. "Please." But the record didn't listen. It went straight through the door and into the kitchen.

Ade dropped the other records and as quickly as he could, he climbed the stairs back to his room. He just caught his dad shouting his name as he closed the door.

"Adedoyin Olayiwola Adepitan!"

* * *

Third time lucky, right? Ade thought as he stood on the landing and heard his parents go out into the garden to put out chairs. His next plan was so simple he couldn't believe he hadn't thought of it to begin with.

If no one can find the house, there won't be a party, Ade said to himself. *All I need to do is get rid of the door number.*

He threw his dad's tool belt over his shoulder and crept down the stairs. Ade gently flicked the latch and went outside. There, by the side of the door, was the number Four. All he had to do was take it off the wall and no one would know where number Four Parsons Road was. Job done.

Ade plucked a screwdriver from the belt. It had a flat head, and the screws attaching the number to the wall had a cross in them, but he didn't think that would be a problem. *A screwdriver is a screwdriver*.

He could just about reach the top screw. He stretched up and put the bright red screwdriver in and turned.

Nothing.

He grabbed the screwdriver with both hands and really turned.

Nothing.

He jiggled the screwdriver this way and that to try to loosen the screw.

Nothing.

He got the green hammer out of the belt and hammered the screwdriver in as much as he could, and then turned it.

Nothing.

Ade trudged back up to his room, undid the straps on his caliper, crawled under the covers of his bed and curled up into a ball. That was plan number four. *Maybe everyone will forget about me,* he thought. *Maybe I'm a superhero who can make myself disappear.* Ade bit his lip. He'd forgotten. Superheroes didn't look like him.

CHAPTER 4

THE PARTY

"DOYIN! DOYIN! Come down. Everyone wants to see you."

Ade didn't know how many hours he'd spent sulking beneath his sheets before the party had started. Now it had begun, it was clear this party was probably going to be the loudest that Parsons Road had ever seen.

Uncle Sobanjo had been the first to arrive with his speakers and amplifier, and before long Ade heard the familiar rhythmic drums, melodic guitar and hypnotic vocals of King Sunny Ade, one of his dad's favourite artists. Soon, the whole house seemed to be dancing to the rhythm.

"Now, Doyin!" Mum yelled.

Uh-oh. What if she comes up and carries me down? Ade frowned. *What if the boys from the street see?*

He had no choice. Taking a deep breath, he pulled the sheets back and got himself ready to go downstairs. *Time to face the music.* Slowly, he buckled the straps of his caliper around his left thigh and then his knee. Then he put on his sokoto and agbada, which were white with blue, orange and red swirly patterns dotted all over them, and took one last look at himself in the mirror.

The iron rods from his caliper were showing. They ended in a tiny 'L' shape and slotted into holes in the heel of his hospital boot on his left leg. Ade covered them as best as he could, but it wasn't much good. It was obvious that he was wearing something strange on his leg; there was just no hiding it.

He took a deep breath and headed down the stairs and into the hallway. The party was a sea of people flowing through his house.

Uncles, aunties, cousins and family friends, all with huge smiles on their faces, swooped down on Ade. Their warm hugs and compliments about how nice he looked relaxed him a little but Ade was still scanning his surroundings. *Where are the boys that Mum invited?* he asked himself.

Ade grinned, the knots in his stomach suddenly gone. *They're not coming! Of course they're not!* He grabbed some food and went into the front room.

Munching on a chicken drumstick, he watched one of his cousins dancing. It looked like fun, so he got up to join her. Then Ade saw them through the window: the three boys he'd seen playing football on Parsons Road. They were standing right in front of his house. There were two teenagers with them, a stocky boy and a tall girl, who he didn't recognise.

As Ade stared at them, the girl suddenly started laughing and pointed down the street. Ade felt his chest tighten. Walking towards his house, Ade saw his auntie and uncle, Mr and Mrs Okolie. They looked fantastic in their traditional Nigerian clothes, but Ade realised that the older boy and girl didn't see that.

The three younger boys didn't join in with the laughter. They just looked at their feet.

As Ade's uncle and aunt got closer, the older boy began making grunting noises and scratching under his armpits. Then he started hopping up and down from one foot to the other. The girl thought this was really funny and laughed even harder.

"Go home monkeys!" she shouted in between fits of giggles. "Ooo-ooo-ooo."

Ade's heart started pounding hard. In his mind, he was back in Queen's Market facing those horrible men. The same thing seemed to be happening again, only this time it was on his street, in the place where his family had made their home.

Ade shook his head. *Why are there so many angry people in this country?* His hands curled into fists. *Maybe I'll get angry as well.* He marched to the front door and yanked it open just as his aunt and uncle arrived.

Uncle had his arms around his wife. It was as if he were trying to protect her from the teenagers' words. Ade saw the sadness on his auntie's face, but as soon as she saw Ade her eyes lit up.

"This is the young man we've come to see." She gave him a huge hug. "Look how much you've grown."

Uncle smiled and shook Ade's hand. "How are you?" he asked.

"I'm fine, Uncle," said Ade, looking down the path at the kids standing outside the front garden. He could see that the girl and the boy were still chuckling. "Please come in. Mum and Dad can't wait to see you."

Ade's aunt and uncle smiled and made their way into the house.

Ade stared at the kids. Fear fought with anger. Five against one were not good odds if things turned nasty. Ade gritted his teeth and strode to the front gate, not caring that he was wearing Nigerian clothes and that everyone could see his caliper.

"What do *you* want?" the tall girl snarled as Ade approached.

"Yeah. Go back to your monkeys' tea party, Peg Leg!" the older boy shouted.

"Why don't you shut your stupid fat mouth!" Ade's anger made his voice much louder than even he expected and once he started, he couldn't stop. "I've seen real monkeys and they're amazing and intelligent creatures, unlike you and your stupid friends!"

There was a stunned silence. The boy's mouth opened and closed like a fish. His hands curled into fists as he stared at Ade.

Ade was shaking. His heart was pounding so hard it felt like it was trying to escape his chest. *He's going to punch me,* Ade thought. *It's going to hurt.*

CHAPTER 5

THE PARSONS ROAD GANG

The teenager took a step forwards, fist raised, but a voice stopped him.

"Do you know what the difference is between monkeys and apes?" the voice said. It came from a tall, skinny boy wearing blue-rimmed glasses. He had Afro hair shaped into a box cut, which made him look even taller. He came to stand next to Ade but didn't wait for an answer to his question and continued as if he were a teacher giving a lesson. "Monkeys have tails and apes don't, and the whole of the human race evolved from apes, hundreds of thousands of years ago."

Ade blinked, unsure quite what to make of this development.

The teenage boy and the girl frowned.

"Shut up, Brian," said the older boy. "You and Peg Leg may be monkeys, but we're not."

The teenage girl nodded. "Come on, let's go before we're bored to death. We'll leave Monkey Boy and Four Eyes to it."

The teenagers turned to leave, but the two other boys stayed where they were.

"Nah, you're alright, Deano," said the small boy with bright ginger hair. "We're gonna stay right here with Brian."

The boy next to him, who was as wide as he was tall, nodded.

"Fine. Suit yourselves," Deano replied.

"Come on, Sam, I've got better things to do than waste my time talking to these mugs!"

Deano and Sam walked off making monkey sounds as they went.

Ade narrowed his eyes as he watched them go. He turned to the three boys still stood by his house. *Why had they stayed? Do they want trouble?* He looked each of them in the eye, daring them to say something. It reminded him of a western he'd watched with his dad. The first person to flinch or back down loses, and it wasn't going to be him.

The boy with the blue-rimmed glasses stuck out a welcoming hand. "I'm Brian. I'm the brains around here, but you probably guessed that."

Ade shook his hand. "Hi," he said, trying to make his voice sound deeper. "My name's Ade."

"Don't listen to Brian, Ade!" shouted the boy with ginger hair. "He only thinks he's the brains. I'm Dexter Trimmingham the Third. I've got the best right foot in East London." To prove his point, Dexter swung his right foot wildly in Ade's direction as if he were blasting a football past him.

"I'm Shezhad," mumbled the last boy. "But everyone calls me Shed."

Ade looked Shed up and down. He really was huge.

"Sorry about my cousin." Dexter shuffled from side to side. "Deano's not always like that, honestly. Sometimes he's really nice."

"Oh yeah, like that time he helped those ants sunbathe by using a magnifying glass." Brian rolled his eyes.

Shed chuckled to himself then looked away because everyone had turned to look at him.

"Shut it, Brian." Dexter's face was turning apple red. "You know his family are going through a tough time."

Ade decided to change the subject. "Who's the girl?"

"Samantha Pringle," said Dexter. "She's Deano's girlfriend. Deano's only just turned 13, but she's 14 and she–"

Dexter broke off as Ade's mum came rushing out of the house.

"Are you okay, Doyin?" she said, slightly out of breath. "Your auntie said you came out here on your own."

Ade looked at the three boys. They all seemed a little confused and he thought he knew why.

"My full name's Adedoyin," he explained to them. "Some people call me Doyin."

"Oh!" they said as one.

"I'm fine, Mum." Ade kind of wished she'd go inside. Having just stood up to Deano and Sam on his own, the last thing he wanted the others to think was that he only did it because he knew his mum was coming out to help him.

Dexter stepped forwards and said, "Hi, Ade's mum, I'm Dexter Trimmingham the Third, and these are my friends Brian and Shed."

"Pleased to meet you all," Ade's mum replied. "But what are you doing out here?"

"Oh, well, you see, you invited us." Brian pushed his glasses up his nose. "Didn't you?"

Ade's mum laughed. "What I mean is, come inside and have something to eat. We've got chicken, plantain and jollof rice – it's only a little spicy."

Ade gaped at her. *A little bit spicy!?* The jollof rice was his cousin's speciality and Dad called it dragon fuel. The last time Ade had tried some he'd had to sit for two hours with ice cubes in his mouth. *What if one of the boys combusted from eating the food?* He could see the headlines in the papers: DEATH

BY JOLLOF: Three young British boys explode after eating Cousin Remi's fiery jollof rice!

Thankfully, Ade's fears were unfounded. Due largely to the three boys witnessing another of Ade's cousins in agony after one spoonful of the rice and rushing to the kitchen to drink 15 glasses of water.

They tucked into the chicken and plantain instead and couldn't get enough of it.

"Great party!" all three of the boys said in unison.

"Thank you," Ade replied. He'd been so worried about them coming but it was actually okay. *Things seem much worse when you're imagining them*, he realised. *But when you confront the reality, it's really not that bad at all.*

"What are those clothes you're wearing?" Dexter asked.

That was the sort of question Ade had been dreading earlier in the day, but now he replied proudly, "They're traditional Nigerian clothes."

Dexter looked intrigued. "Where's Nigeria?" he asked.

"Well, you take a left after Queen's Market," Ade began. "Then head up Green Street and it's just next to the pie 'n' mash shop."

Dexter scratched his head, trying to work out if he'd seen this mysterious place called Nigeria.

Brian laughed. "Nigeria is in West Africa, you silly sausage!"

Dexter screwed up his eyes. "I knew that, I'm not stupid!" Then, a moment later, he said, "Where's Africa?"

This time Shed, Brian and Ade all started laughing.

Shed pointed to Ade's leg and the metal rods going into his boot. "So, are you a robot or something?" he asked.

Ade opened his mouth to explain that he'd had polio and how his caliper supported his left leg so he could walk.

"Obviously, he's a robot!" Dexter said first. He started making strange mechanical noises and walking stiffly around the corridor with his arms rigid by his sides.

Shed chuckled as Dexter pretended he was a malfunctioning robot and bumped into the wall.

"WHO PUT THIS HERE? DESTROY, DESTROY!" Dexter sounded just like a dalek from *Doctor Who*.

Brian put down his plate of food. "He's not a robot, he's a cyborg!"

"Am I?" Ade questioned.

"Yeah, a cyborg is a human with mechanical enhancements that give them super-strength," Brian said knowingly.

"AWESOME!" said Dexter.

"Super-strength," Ade said. "Sounds good to me."

"That means you can play football, right?" Shed asked.

"Of course I can!" Then he turned to Dexter and said cheekily, "I've got the best left foot in East London."

Shed nudged Brian and gave him a look as if he wanted him to say something. But before Brian could say a word, Dexter stepped forwards and announced, "We're the Parsons Road Gang. We don't cause trouble, we just love playing football and we could do with a player with super-cyborg-strength. Wanna join our team?"

Ade felt tingly with happiness but told himself to be cool. "Yeah, I'll join your team."

"Great," said Brian. "We'll call for you tomorrow morning. We can work on our skills."

"Hey, why are we waiting till tomorrow to play football?" Ade asked. "Let's play in my garden."

"What, now?" asked Brian.

"Yes," Ade said. "Right now."

CHAPTER 6

SUPER-STRENGTH

The great thing about football is that if you've got a ball you don't really need much else. In fact, sometimes you don't even need a ball. Ade had played many matches with a scrunched-up piece of paper and even a plastic cup.

Thankfully, though, this time Ade did have a ball. His claret-and-blue one was already outside in the small back garden. His dad had bought it for him from a shop in Upton Park.

"Whoa! Is that a West Ham football?" Brian's eyes were wide.

"It's a real-life, actual Mitre Pro 2000!" Dexter charged forwards, the ball a magnet that couldn't be resisted.

Ade, Shed and Dexter chased after him. Ade knew he wasn't as quick as his new friends. His heavy caliper slowed him down and the iron rods meant he couldn't bend his left leg either, which meant he didn't move in the same way as the others. Ade shrugged. *It's never stopped me before,* he thought. *And it won't stop me now.*

As the game went on, Ade noticed Shed looking at him. He was watching Ade's heavy limp and how he favoured his right side because he had more strength there.

He doesn't think I can keep up. Ade pushed away his annoyance, but when Shed passed the ball to him with the feeblest cross *ever*, Ade knew he had to say something. *People don't understand things they haven't seen before*, he reminded himself. To his friends and family in Nigeria he was just plain old Ade. But Shed, Brian and Dexter had never seen anybody like him. Aside from his leg, he also dressed differently and had a strange accent.

As the ball approached, Ade knew this would be the first of many tests. All he really wanted was to be like everybody else and fit in, but to do that he would have to prove he wasn't any different from the other kids. *I have to show them.*

He maneuvered himself so the ball came towards his strong right foot. Then he blasted it as hard as he could towards Dexter. As the ball flew towards him like an arrow, Dexter just had time to open his mouth in amazement before it hit him on the forehead and then spun off in the air.

"TIIIMBEEER," Brian yelled.

Dexter fell to the ground with his arms open wide.

"Sorry, mate!" Ade yelled as the rest of the boys cracked up.

They finally managed to stop laughing but it was hard because Dexter was now pretending to be dazed and walking around in dizzy circles.

Shed shook his head. "Amazing shot."

Brian came over and put his arm around Ade's shoulders. He looked at Shed and Dexter and said, "I told you he had super-strength." He said 'super-strength' slowly and quietly as if it was their secret.

"Ah! shut up!" Ade said, trying to hide his smile. "Come on, let's play football."

Shed and Ade looked at each other. Then they both raced towards the ball, which was at the far end of the garden. Shed got to it first. He tried to dribble past Ade, but Ade called on his super-strength and slid into him with a crunching tackle.

They both fell to the ground in a heap. Brian and Dexter jumped on top of them in a classic bundle. Ade ended up underneath Shed and was laughing so hard it took him a minute to realise that someone was shouting his name.

"DOYIN! DOYIN!"

Uh-oh, Mum.

"Arrrgh! Adedoyin Olayiwola Adepitan!" she shouted again. "What *are* you doing? Your agbada and sokoto are going to get filthy!"

The boys rolled off Ade quick-fast.

Ade sat up and brushed down his outfit. The mud wasn't budging. Mum shook her head.

"I think it's time for us to go." Brian got to his feet.

Dexter nodded. "Yeah, my mum will be expecting me."

Ade felt sad that his new friends were leaving. He slowly started to stand up. As he did so, a big hand grabbed his arm and helped him to his feet. It was Shed.

"Great tackle," he said, smiling.

That made Ade feel good.

The boys headed back into the house and towards the front door, passing the room in which Ade's dad had just moved to the centre. The beat kicked in and a loud whoop came from Dad. "Come on, everybody, give me some space. Let me show you amateurs how it's done!"

With all the aunties and uncles clapping and cheering, he started pointing at them and gyrating as if he were being electrocuted, before screaming at the top of his voice, "Hee! Hee! Oh yeah, now that's how we do it in Lagos."

Ade stared at his father in horror and then at his friends. Brian, Dexter and Shed were transfixed. Ade felt sick. He'd just made new friends and Dad was going to ruin it all with his crazy dance moves. *What if he attempts The Worm?* Ade thought. *It'll be a disaster.*

Brian turned to Ade. "Mine does that as well," he sighed. "Loves doing The Funky Chicken. It's terrible."

Ade laughed, mainly out of relief. He didn't know what The Funky Chicken was, but everyone knew chickens couldn't dance.

"We'll see you tomorrow." Dexter waved as he headed off on the short journey to his house next door.

"Yeah, see you tomorrow, Ade," said Brian and Shed, walking in the opposite direction. They lived next to each other two doors up from Ade's house.

Ade shut the door. His face ached from smiling so much. He heard the phone ring in the hallway. Mum answered it.

"How many mice?" she asked. "A hundred?!"

Ade could feel Mum's glare boring into his back, but he was already rushing into the front room, planning to lose himself in the crowd.

"Hey, Dad," he shouted. "Make room for me. Let's do The Worm!"

CHAPTER 7

FOOTBALL, FOOTBALL AND MORE FOOTBALL

"Slow down," Mum said. "You'll give yourself indigestion eating your breakfast so fast."

Ade stuffed some more toast in his mouth and strained to listen for the doorbell. What if he missed Dexter, Shed and Brian calling for him? *They might think I've changed my mind, about everything – playing football, joining the Parsons Road*

Gang, being their friend. They'll head off without me and never invite me to play with them again.

He swallowed the last piece of toast and ran to the window. There was still no sign of them, so he went up to his bedroom and paced around. Now all sorts of other thoughts started running through Ade's head. Maybe they'd decided he was just too strange to have as a friend: the way he walked, his accent, his crazy family. Even though they'd had great fun at the party, after having had some time to think about it they now probably didn't want to have anything to do with hi–

DING DONG!

Ade ran out of his room and slid down the banister on his tummy. (Sliding down the banisters was something he'd perfected since being in England.) He landed at the bottom of the stairs just before his mum, who was also heading to the door.

"It's okay, I've got this," he said, slightly out of breath.

Ade's mum gave him a disapproving frown. *She's probably still upset about how quickly I ate breakfast... and the mice.*

Ade opened the door to find Dexter, Shed and Brian standing in his front garden, all with cheesy grins on their faces.

"Are you coming out or what?" Dexter sounded impatient.

Using his index finger, Brian pushed his blue-rimmed glasses from the end of his nose back up his face. He smiled. "It's time to see how good you really are, Ade."

"As long as he doesn't celebrate scoring goals by dancing like his dad we'll be okay," Shed chipped in.

"Cyborgs don't dance they just win," Ade replied. "Come on, let's go."

The boys all laughed and ran onto Parsons Road.

It was hot. Ade's new friends were wearing shorts and football tops. Ade was not. Even though it was very warm, he didn't really want the others to see the caliper on his left leg, so he was wearing a pair of bright blue tracksuit bottoms. Cyborg or not, he still felt a little self-conscious about the way he looked.

The others didn't seem to have noticed though, or if they had they weren't saying anything. It didn't take long before Ade forgot about his caliper, his tracksuit bottoms and his self-consciousness, and just started having fun.

They played all day and then, the next morning, they did it all over again. And then the next day and the next.

Out on the pitch, Ade knew he was okay. He was a good passer, and a demon tackler, but he struggled with running. When he was in goal, though, everything changed. Ade could catch and save anything that came at him, even from close range. He was fearless!

"You know what?" Brian said one afternoon. "I'm not going to call you Ade or Doyin any more. You're Cyborg Cat."

"Cyborg Cat?" Ade repeated.

"Yeah," Dexter said. "Because you have the reflexes of a cat. It's one of your superpowers."

Ade grinned. He loved superheroes. He loved that his friends thought he was one.

Ade had actually needed superpowers for the length of the game they'd just played. It had ended 108-107, though no one was

quite sure if that was right as they'd sort of lost count after goal number 100.

He lay on his back having a rest. *This is the best summer of my life*, he thought. The horrible men in Queen's Market seemed a long time ago now, even though the memory of that day did creep up on him sometimes. *But I'm not the same scared little boy who shut myself away from the world.*

"Oi!" a deep voice yelled.

Ade felt a surge of fear. He sat up.

"Look what you've done to my tomatoes," Mr Smoothhead from up the road cried. He pointed a finger at the Parsons Road Gang. "Next time I see that ball in my garden I'll put a hole in it the size of the Blackwall Tunnel, you little bleeders!"

"Sorry," the boys said as one.

Dexter pulled them into a huddle. "Listen. There's a place, a secret place, where we can play football on proper grass with proper goal posts, and away from grumps like Mr Smoothhead. My brother told me about it the other day."

"So why are you just telling us now?" Brian demanded.

Dexter glanced at Ade's caliper. "It's a bit too far to walk. We'd have to go there on our bikes."

Ade sighed deeply. "Well that's no good for me, is it?" The other three looked at him. Ade could tell they were embarrassed. *They think I'm going to say something about my leg.* "I don't have a bike!"

Dexter punched Ade on the shoulder. "Joker."

Shed grinned. "No problem, you can jump on the back of mine."

"Great," Ade said. "Problem solved. Tomorrow we'll saddle up and head off to the secret football pitch."

CHAPTER 8

SILLY SAUSAGES AND BROKEN DREAMS

Ade's friends arrived even earlier than usual that morning. Shed was on his bright red three-speed Raleigh Chopper, Dexter had a chrome BMX Diamondback and Brian had a blue six-speed racing bike.

"Ready?" Shed asked.

Ade nodded and climbed onto the back of Shed's Chopper. His caliper scraped against the back wheel of the bike, even though it was covered up by his tracksuit bottoms. Ade tried to ignore it. "Come on, let's go!"

"Wait a second," Brian said. "You definitely got the sausages, Dex?"

"Yep, sausages packed." Dexter pushed down hard on his pedals and set off, followed by Brian.

"Why do we need to bring sausages?" Ade asked.

Shed shrugged. "I guess we'll find out." He pedalled after the other two.

Ade held on tight and watched the houses on Parsons Road fly by. He saw snapshots that now felt familiar and comforting to him: kids playing out front, Dexter's older brother with his mates trying to fix up a car, women on the front step talking about what was on TV last night.

"Woof, woof... grrr... woof... woof."

Hang on, Ade thought as they got to the top of the road. *That sound is not familiar or comforting.*

A huge Alsatian leapt over a garden wall and started chasing the boys.

"IT'S KING!" Dexter cried. "See, Brian, I told you he was big."

Brian quickly glanced back. "Whoa, he's huge!" His feet and the pedals became a blur.

"Faster, faster," screamed Ade. He was no fool. Sitting on the back of Shed's bike meant he'd be King's first course if the dog caught up with them.

Shed stood up and pedalled even harder to try to get away.

"Sausages!" he screamed as they whizzed past Dexter.

"I'm trying," Dexter cried, his fingers fumbling about in his coat pocket. He'd slowed right down and King was directly behind him now, teeth gnashing.

"THROW THE SAUSAGES, YOU SILLY SAUSAGE!" Brian yelled from the front.

Ade wished he could morph into Cyborg Cat right now. He'd pluck Dexter from his bike and bound to safety. But Dexter didn't need a superhero. He needed a distraction. Pulling a string of raw, fat Wall's sausages from his pocket, he hurled them at the dog. They soared through the air like some sort of weird flying caterpillar and were caught about six feet from the ground by the ravenous creature. With a yelp of pleasure, King completely forgot about the boys and greedily chomped down on the sausages.

"Woo hoo! Nice work Dexter!" Ade yelled.

"Talk about leaving it to the last minute," Brian reprimanded from the front.

"Rubbish," said Dexter. "I had the situation under complete control. Come on!"

He took the lead once more and they zoomed forwards, only stopping once they arrived at a place called Southern Road Playing Fields.

It was just as Dexter had described it - a full-size football pitch with huge goals and beautiful well-cut and well-maintained grass. Even the markings on the pitch looked beautiful to the boys. Ade couldn't wait to put a ball on the bright white penalty spot and take a shot at goal.

"I can't believe it," Ade breathed. "Why isn't anyone else here?"

"A local team used to play on the pitch," explained Dexter, "but they went bankrupt and had to leave. The caretaker, Mr James, loves his job though, so he keeps it in good condition."

"But doesn't he mind when people use it?" asked Shed.

"Nah," said Dexter. "He told my brother he's fine with people using it as long as there's no litter and no trouble."

"Oi, stop yakking, you two," shouted Brian, moving along the fence to a hole big enough for them to get through. "It's time for kick-off."

The boys played all morning and then flopped down on the grass to wolf down lunch.

"Let's have another penalty competition after this," said Dexter in between bites of peanut butter sandwich.

"Waste of time," said Shed. "I'll only win again."

"Not a chance," snorted Brian. "You only won before because Dex burped and put me off on my last penalty."

"So how come you missed the other three before that?" Shed replied, laughing.

"Listen," interjected Ade. "None of you are going to win, because I'm going to save every one of your penalties."

"Yeah?" said Dexter. "We'll see about that."

The boys dropped their sandwiches. It was clearly time for the rematch.

Ade got in goal. Brian went first and scored three of his five penalties, followed by Dexter, who scored three as well.

Ade had hurled himself through the air as if they were playing on marshmallows rather than grass. He loved it, despite the fact that the goals were gigantic compared to him. He really had managed to pull off some spectacular saves.

Now the pressure was all on Shed.

He put the ball on the penalty spot and stepped back what seemed like miles. Ade rolled his eyes. Clearly, Shed favoured a very long run-up.

"Watch and learn my friends." He charged towards the ball and unleashed a humungous shot. Ade lunged to his right as the ball went flying over the bar and landed about 30 metres behind the goal.

Brian and Dexter cracked up laughing. "We were watching but we didn't learn much!"

Ade tried not to chuckle too much at Shed's expression.

"I'll go and get it, shall I?" Ade ran towards the ball, when suddenly his caliper started making a funny noise.

He stopped for a moment and then took another step.

CLUNK!

He took another step.

PING!

He looked down just in time to see a screw roll down his trouser leg and land on the grass. Ade frowned and stared at the small shiny object, but before he'd had time to work out fully what was happening, he heard a snapping sound. "Oh no!"

The other three boys came running over. "What's the matter?" asked Shed.

"I think my caliper's broken," said Ade. "The rod's snapped." He tried to put pressure on his left leg, but the mechanism gave way and he crumpled to the ground.

He lay on the floor, his heartbeat pounding in his ears. Without his caliper, he couldn't walk. How was he going to get

home? The bikes were at the other end of the field.

What are the boys going to think, when they realise I can't walk any more? Or play football? Ade bit his lip. *What will they think once they realise I don't really have super-strength and I'm just a useless boy who can't even stand on his own leg?*

Ade could feel the tears starting to build as he imagined his friends walking away and leaving him there, helpless. Surely they wouldn't want to be friends with him now?

That's when he felt something under his arms.

"Don't worry, we've got you," said Brian.

Ade felt himself being lifted up off the ground. He looked to his side and saw that he had his arms around Brian and Dexter's shoulders. They had helped him up.

"Come on, get on."

Ade looked in front of him. It was Shed. He'd knelt down ready for Ade to get on his back.

Ade hopped on and Shed gave him a piggyback all the way to the bikes.

They didn't say much on the ride home, which thankfully didn't include another meeting with King. When they got to Ade's house, the other three all helped him to his doorstep. Ade sat down and looked at his friends.

"Thanks," he said.

"Hey, we're the Parsons Road Gang," said Brian. "We stick together through thick and thin."

"Yeah," Shed said. He took a step back and, in dramatic American TV presenter style, said, "He is the bionic man! We can rebuild him!"

Even Ade smiled a little at that one.

"See you, Ade," said Brian. "You made some great saves today."

"Yeah, see you, Cyborg Cat," said Dexter.

Ade held up a hand. "See you."

CHAPTER 9

MR TOWERS

"Tut, tut, tut."

Mr Towers pursed lips as he scratched the bald patch neatly sandwiched between two tufts of hair on his head. To Ade, he sounded like a very old car backfiring and, even though he knew he shouldn't laugh at the head technician at Great Ormond Street Hospital, he struggled not to giggle.

Mr Towers peered at Ade from beneath eyebrows that were extremely bushy. He was smartly dressed in a suit and bow tie, with a technician's coat on top. Ade knew Mr Towers was in charge of making all the appliances used by disabled children, but somehow he looked more like Mr. Potato Head. This didn't help him with the giggles.

Ade looked over at Mum and Dad to see if they were laughing. They were not. They looked really worried and suddenly, Ade's giggles evaporated.

"You've well and truly broken it," Mr Towers said, picking up the pieces of Ade's caliper.

"Can you fix it, though?" Dad asked. "My son's due to start at Credon Primary School in two weeks' time. Without his caliper that's not going to happen."

Mr Towers rubbed his chin. "I'm afraid it's not straightforward."

Dad pinched the bridge of his nose and Mum bit her lip. Ade knew they'd spent a long time trying to convince the local school to take him on as a pupil. Apparently, all the schools in East London were worried that Ade wouldn't be able to cope with the stairs. Ade couldn't really understand why. Playing football with the Parsons Road Gang had made him super fit, but if the school were worried it made Ade feel worried.

Mr Towers held the broken caliper above his head, looking it up and down carefully. "Thing is, this screw is easily replaced," he said. "But this part here has completely snapped." Mr Towers pointed to the L-shaped part of the caliper that slotted into Ade's boots.

Ade's mum and dad looked at each other. That really didn't sound like good news.

"But, erm, can you fix it Mr Towers?"

Mum repeated the question. They were desperate to know the answer.

"Oh, yes, of course it can be fixed," replied Mr Towers. "Everything can be fixed."

Ade felt a flash of excitement. Then disappointment. He wanted his caliper back, he'd really missed playing football these last few days with his mates, but he didn't really want to start school. *Sure, my friends will be there, but what will everyone else be like?*

Ade's parents were looking much happier. Ade could almost see the worry leaving their bodies, like air from a balloon.

"Yes," Mr Towers said. "We'll have it as good as new for you in about six weeks."

"Six weeks!" Ade's dad exclaimed. "But what about school?"

"It's gonna be all right Dad," Ade said. "It doesn't matter if I start school a few weeks late. You and Mum can teach me at home."

Why didn't I think of that before? Ade thought. *It's the perfect solution.* He didn't want to go to school at all. *What if the other kids were like Deano and Sam or, even worse, the horrible men in Queen's Market?* Ade imagined himself arriving in the school playground with hundreds of kids staring and laughing at the way he walked. He could practically hear all the children whispering and giggling and then, as more and more joined in, they all started shouting and pointing, "Go back to your own country, Peg Leg! Nobody wants you here; go home!"

He began to shake.

"Ade? Ade? Are you okay?"

Ade blinked and realised Mr Towers, his mum and his dad, were all staring at him. He wiped the sweat from his forehead. "Oh yeah, yeah, I'm okay."

Mr Towers frowned and turned to Ade's parents. "Look, I can see how upset your son is about this," he said to them. "I can't promise anything, Mr and Mrs Adepitan, but I'll have a word with a few people and see if we can speed things up a little. With any luck, we may be able to get the repair time down to three weeks."

Ade groaned to himself. Somehow, he'd made things worse and he'd be starting school sooner rather than later now.

Mum was beaming and Dad looked like he wanted to hug Mr Towers.

Luckily, Mr Towers distracted him. "Oh, and one more thing. To save you having to carry Ade around while we fix his caliper,

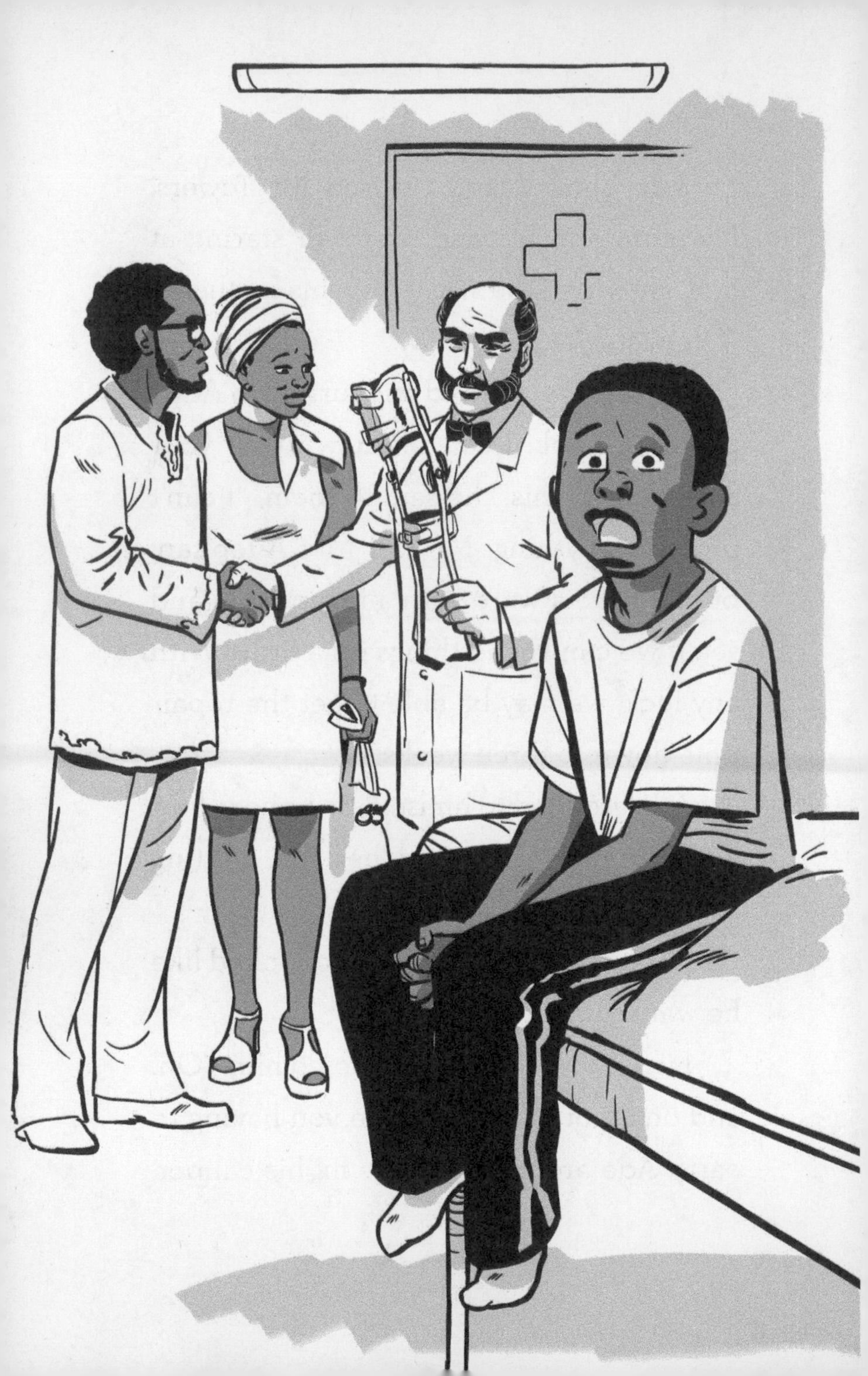

I've arranged for him to have a wheelchair. You can pick it up on your way out."

Ade wrinkled his nose. He hated wheelchairs and hated the whole idea of using one. *Wheelchairs are for really disabled people who can't even play football*, he thought. *Now, I'm going to be one of them.*

CHAPTER 10

IN A BIT OF A FIX

Brian paced up and down Ade's bedroom, rubbing his chin and thinking. It must have been something he'd seen on television and he was probably doing it because he thought it made him seem even more intelligent. Ade wasn't so sure. *Why would walking back and forth give you cleverer thoughts than if you were just sitting down and thinking?*

Brian wasn't the only one thinking, though. Shed was sitting on the end of

Ade's bed, bouncing a rubber ball off the floor and onto the wall as he pondered their problem, and Dexter was trying to balance on his head with his legs up against the bedroom door. He claimed it really did help him think better and was something he always did when the gang had a big problem to solve.

And boy did they have a big problem to solve! A big, buggy shaped problem.

"Why a buggy?" Dexter asked, still upside down. "Why won't your parents let you use the wheelchair?"

Ade sighed. He wanted to explain but he wasn't sure Dex would get it. Life was really hard for disabled people in Nigeria. There were very few opportunities for them and, for the most part, they were only ever seen begging in the streets. Ade knew his parents had come to the UK because they wanted him to be independent and have the best life possible. *They haven't come here to see me in a wheelchair and they don't want me to rely on one. To them that looks like I'm properly disabled. And they're right. Walking with my caliper is best.*

"They just don't like it," Ade said instead. "But they need to get me around somehow."

Dexter was going red in the face so flopped down on the floor. "Well, mate, being pushed around in a buggy is doing nothing for your reputation. A wheelchair would be much better."

Brian glared at him and Dexter shrugged. "I'm just saying."

Ade flopped back on his bed. "I need my caliper back, and fast."

"Definitely," Brian said. "School's starting soon."

Ade shook his head. "I don't care about that. I don't want to go to school; it's going to be horrible."

"No it won't," Shed promised. "We're the Parsons Road Gang and we always stick together." He threw the ball against the wall again, but this time it ricocheted past Shed's outstretched hand and hit Brian on the side of his head.

All the boys started laughing, apart from Brian who was anxiously examining his specs. "You could have broken my glasses. You know I can't see a thing without them."

"Chill out, Brian, it was an accident," Ade said. "Nothing's broken and nothing needs to be fixed."

"Hang on. That's it," Brian shouted. "I've got it!"

"Yes, we know you've got it. The worse case of flatulence known to man," Ade replied.

The boys cracked up laughing again. One of Brian's favourite meals was eggs and beans with loads of ketchup. He claimed the protein in the eggs helped him to think clearly. The problem was, they also gave him horrible wind.

"No, you sausages!" Brian spoke fast, something he did when he was about to come up with a clever idea. "Shed, your cousin Abdul is a mechanic, right?"

Shed looked confused, but nodded. "Sort of," he said. "He actually welds cars back together after they've been in accidents. He fixed my bike really well last summer. Made it better, actually."

Dexter jumped to his feet. "Abdul could fix Ade's caliper! Brian, you're a genius!"

"Correct," said Brian. "I am a genius. And yes, correct again, Abdul is the answer to our problem."

Dexter and Brian jumped in the air and chest-bumped each other in celebration. Then they did the Parsons Road Gang special handshake, which involved linking thumbs and wiggling all the other fingers.

"Hang on," Ade said. "Mr Towers has my caliper. There's no way he's going to give it to us to fix."

Everyone's face fell and Brian began to pace again. He was pacing for a while, ages in fact, and then he stopped. "Well, they say the pen is mightier than the sword."

"Who says that?" Dexter looked confused.

Brian frowned. "The 'who' doesn't matter."

"What he's saying is that we should write Mr Towers a letter, right?" Ade said.

Brian nodded. "We'll write him a letter and say that Abdul can fix the caliper." Brian spread his arms wide. "He'll thank us. We're essentially taking work off his hands."

Shed grinned. "Great, and then we can all start school together."

Ade pursed his lips. He really wanted his caliper back but the idea of starting school still filled him with fear.

"Come on," Brian said. "Let's write this letter." He ripped the top sheet from a nearby pad of paper and handed it to Ade. "You should write it. It will mean more coming from you."

Ade nodded and began to write:

Der Mr Towers. I wood reely like it if you cud send bak my clipper so Abdul can ficks it. Tank you veery mush. Ade

Brian read it over his shoulder. "Well, it's definitely a unique letter. Now it just needs to be post–"

"Boys, time for you to go," Ade's mum called up. "Your parents will be wondering where you are."

"Don't worry," Ade said. "Leave it to me. I know where the stamps and envelopes are kept and my mum's address book."

The boys did their secret handshake.

"Let me know if you need me," Shed said. "We can take it to the postbox together."

"Will do."

After dinner, Ade found the stamps. He licked the back of one and stuck it on the envelope. Ade chuckled to himself as he did so. *It's actually pretty gross*, he

thought. *It's like licking the back of the Queen's head or something.* He didn't think she'd like that very much if anyone did it for real. *Now there's only one thing left to do,* Ade thought. *Post the letter. Shed said he'd help.*

"Mum," shouted Ade. "Can I go round to Shed's? I need to show him something."

"Yes," Mum said. "But only a quick visit. It's bedtime soon. Do you want me to take you in the buggy?"

"**NO!**" Ade shouted. "It's not far. I can get there."

A few minutes later, Ade turned up on Shed's doorstep dripping with sweat.

"What happened to you?" Shed asked.

"I hopped all the way round," Ade replied.

"You should have just called me, you doughnut." Shed shook his head.

"Come on, let's go post this letter." Ade held the envelope aloft, brandishing it like it was the FA Cup.

The nearest postbox was five streets away and by the time they got there, Shed was the one who was sweating. He'd given Ade a piggyback all the way.

"This is going to work," said Ade, holding the letter up. "I believe in the power of the Parsons Road Gang."

"Yeah," gasped Shed. "The power of the Parsons Road Gang can make anything happen."

"Here goes." Ade slid the precious letter into the opening of the postbox and held it there for a couple of seconds before letting it go.

Ten minutes later they were back outside Ade's house.

"Thanks, Shed," said Ade as his friend knelt down to let him off his back.

Shed slumped to the ground next to him, exhausted, and just about managed to mumble, "No problem."

"Hey, what's up with you two?"

Ade and Shed looked up. It was Brian.

"Shed just took me to post the letter."

"Right," said Brian, looking at Shed who was breathing heavily and gradually slumped even further down. "But why did he have to take you? Why didn't you just ask him to post the letter for you?"

Ade and Shed looked at each other. They both burst out laughing, realising at the exact same moment how silly they'd been.

When they'd calmed down, Ade looked at his friends and said, "I believe in the power of the Parsons Road Gang."

"Yeah," said Shed. "It's so strong, I'll bet we'll get your caliper back and fixed by tomorrow."

CHAPTER 11

NO TIME TO LOSE

Ade's caliper did not arrive for Abdul to fix the next day. Or the one after. Or the one after that. By the middle of the following week, Ade was feeling truly miserable.

He'd been taken out in the buggy three more times. Some people just stared, but others would come up and pat him on the head and say how cute he looked. One woman had even taken a rattle out of her bag and given it to him. Even worse was when a group of kids had started laughing at him and making baby noises.

Ade had told his parents how much he hated the buggy. "Can't I just stay at home until my caliper is fixed?"

His dad was having none of it. "Come on. You're not hiding in this house."

School was due to start in 5 days' time and the other boys were all getting ready. They'd done their best to keep Ade's spirits up, but nothing much was working. Ade didn't want to go to school at all, but if he had to go, he realised that what he really, really didn't want was to start late and turn up when everyone else had settled in. He was going to stick out like a sore thumb anyway, but arriving on his own would make it a hundred times worse.

By the time Friday came around he wished he could just fall asleep and wake up back in Nigeria with the whole thing having been a bad dream. Lying on his bed, he imagined playing with his cousins at Gran-gran's house, running around, looking out for colobus monkeys leaping acrobatically through the trees.

"Doyin! Doyin! Come quickly! Doyin!"

It was his mum. Ade pushed himself off the bed and shuffled downstairs. His mum was running around, putting her coat on and looking for the house keys.

"Mum, what is it?" he asked. "Is everything okay?"

"The hospital called. They said your caliper is ready. If we can get there by five, they can fit it today."

"It's fixed?" Ade said. "But Abdul didn't–"

"Abdul?" repeated his mum. She shook her head. "Doyin, it's almost four, we've got to hurry if they're going to fit it today. Get ready."

Five minutes later, Ade was strapped in the buggy and being pushed to the number 5 bus stop on Barking Road as fast as his mum could go.

Ade heard someone snort with laughter as they arrived.

He closed his eyes. *Why did mum put me in this buggy?*

"Interesting choice of socks," a girl's voice said.

"Huh?" Ade spotted a tall girl with springy hair and golden-brown skin leaning against the bus stop. Her hands were in her tracksuit pockets.

She barely glanced at Ade as she continued, "If you're gonna wear superhero socks, I would go for Iceman; Wolverine is way too obvious."

Still confused, Ade looked down at his bright yellow-and-black socks. His knees were up by his chin as he sat hunched uncomfortably in the baby buggy. Wolverine scowled angrily at Ade from his socks as if he agreed with the strange girl.

"Yup, definitely the wrong choice," the girl said.

Definitely the wrong choice. Ade's heart skipped a beat as he suddenly realised something.

"Wait!" he shouted.

"What, Doyin? What is it?" Mum cried.

"I should be in the wheelchair. Mr Towers gave it to us. What will he think when he sees me in a buggy?"

"Oh, Lord, Doyin, you're right."

Ade's head flew back as Mum tilted the buggy onto its rear wheels and spun it round. As they shot off Ade heard the girl at the bus stop say, "See you later, Wolverine."

She was grinning, her large eyes twinkling with humour.

Ade looked away, not sure how to respond, but it was too late anyway as his mum sprinted back down Parsons Road. They swapped the buggy for the wheelchair and, now even later than they had been before, charged back to the bus stop.

As they waited, Mum went really quiet. *She's nervous*, Ade thought, *and it's not just about us being late. She's worried about getting the wheelchair on the bus.*

He remembered how back in Nigeria the buses were usually old and battered, and crammed full of more people than a tin of sardines who had invited all their friends over to stay. If anyone in a wheelchair had ever tried to get on, the chair would have been strapped to the roof and the person would have been shoved in with everyone else.

On top of that, the drivers drove like maniacs, as if they were Formula One racing drivers in a real hurry.

"Don't worry, Mum," said Ade. "It'll be okay."

Mum nodded and stroked his cheek.

The bus finally arrived and they both breathed a huge sigh of relief. It was fairly empty and there was plenty of room for the wheelchair. A couple of the other passengers even moved seats to make things easier for Ade and his mum. In fact, the only thing she would have liked was for the driver to actually drive like the bus was in a Formula One race.

Ade and his mum spent the whole journey willing cars to get out of the way and telepathically trying to tell the driver to speed up. Whether it worked or not was difficult to know, but they reached their stop at ten to five, got off the bus and raced to Great Ormond Street Hospital.

They burst into the main entrance and headed straight to the lifts.

"Oh no," said Ade's mum. "They're out of order. How am I going to get you to Mr Towers' office on the third floor?"

It looked as if Ade and his mum had come all that way in vain and Ade wasn't going to be able to start school on Monday, after all.

"Can we help you?"

Ade and his mum turned to where the voice had come from and saw two nurses.

"Oh, erm, yes," said Ade's mum. "We need to get to the third floor and the lift is broken."

The nurses looked at each other.

"Come on, young man, up you get."

Ade was just about to say that he couldn't do that, when he felt himself being lifted up

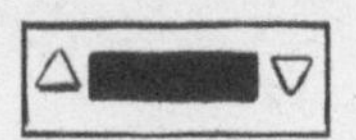

and onto the nurse's shoulders, while the other one folded up the wheelchair and carried it up the stairs.

Ade could feel his nostrils starting to flare; they always did that when he was angry or frustrated. *I don't want their help. I didn't ask for their help. I need to get fitter and stronger, so I can do things by myself.*

"Thank you," Mum said.

The nurse shrugged. "We're just sorry the lifts are broken."

At two minutes to five they were outside Mr Towers' office.

"Ah, you made it," said Mr Towers as Ade and his mum went inside. "Good to see you again. Now then, take a look at this." Mr Towers opened a box and pulled out Ade's caliper.

"Good as new, eh?" he said.

Ade couldn't believe his eyes. It really did look as good as new. Once Mr Towers had fitted the caliper, it turned out it was even better than new. Mr Towers had created a hinge with a lever that allowed Ade to bend his leg at the knee when he was wearing it, something he hadn't been able to do before.

"Thank you so much, Mr Towers," said Mum. "But tell me, how were you able to fix it so quickly?"

"Well," said Mr Towers, looking at Ade. "I received a letter. And, let's just say, reading it made me think that perhaps it would be a good idea for Ade to start school as soon as possible and, when he does, to work very, very hard at his spelling."

CHAPTER 12

PRETTY IN PINK

"Wake up, Doyin. Wake up!"

Ade opened his eyes.

"It's seven thirty," Mum said. "Time to get up for school."

Ade stared at his mum all bleary-eyed.

"Are you okay?" Mum looked concerned. "You were talking in your sleep. You kept on saying, 'No, please no.'"

"Yeah, I'm okay. I just had a bad dream," Ade said. "But I can't quite remember it."

His mum gave him a big hug. "Don't worry, everybody gets nervous on their first day of school." She put her hand on her son's head. "You wait and see, by the end of the afternoon you'll be having such a good time you probably won't want to come home."

Yeah, right. But Mum's warm smile and her reassuring voice made him feel a little better.

"Now, hurry up and get dressed," she said. "Your new suit is all ready for you."

Oh no! The suit. That was what he'd been dreaming about. In that moment, he remembered everything about their trip back to Queen's Market the day before.

Ade hadn't wanted to go. What if they saw those horrible men again? But Mum had said he needed a new outfit for school and there's no arguing with Mum.

It was like he was back at the market...

As soon as they left the house, Ade could feel himself getting anxious. As they approached the actual market, Ade's heart began pounding so hard it felt as if he had a full-on orchestra in his chest. He felt hot and sweaty, and he gripped his mum's hand tightly.

Soon, the familiar sounds of market traders selling their goods started to fill the air. After what had happened the last time they'd been there, Ade was surprised at how calm his mum seemed. She talked and joked with people on the stalls as they wandered round.

Ade felt some tension leave his shoulders. The market felt like a very different place this time, much friendlier, a place where people came to have a good time, not to be shouted at by thugs.

Ade started to spot things he liked the look of and dragged his mum over to a toy stall. *If I play my cards right, I reckon I could get her to buy me something.*

He was playing with a Darth Vader figure, when a deep voice made him jump.

"Come back again, then?"

A chill ran down the back of Ade's neck and he turned. Standing in front of the stall opposite him was a man with a face he recognised, but it wasn't an ugly, snarling one. It was a very round, red, cheery face, and when the man smiled it seemed to double in size and his funny checked hat almost popped off his head.

I remember you, Ade thought. The man was the trader who had looked like he'd wanted to take on the horrible men when they'd started threatening Ade's parents.

"Hello. I'm Glenn Warrick." He extended a massive hand in greeting to Ade's mum. His huge chubby fingers looked just like sausages.

King would love those! Ade thought.

"Just so you know," Glenn went on. "We ain't all like those idiots who were shouting at you that time." His cheeks got even redder. "Sorry you had to go through that. Some people are just wrong'uns!"

For a moment there was silence. Then Ade's mum stretched out a hand to shake his. "Pleased to meet you, Glenn."

She gestured to Ade and gave him a gentle nudge forwards.

"Pleased to meet you, too," said Ade. His hand disappeared inside Glenn's grip and Ade wondered if he'd ever see it again, his hand was so small compared to Glenn's.

"Right, madam, can I interest you in anything in particular?" He pointed proudly at his stall, which was heaving with a vast array of trousers, blazers, jumpers and suits, all neatly laid out or dangling from hangers.

Ade's mum cast her wily shopper's gaze over his goods.

"I'll tell you what I'll do," Glenn said. "You can have a special discount on anything you like today. Twenty per cent off just for you, Mrs...?"

"Mrs Adepitan," she said.

"Righto," said Glenn. "And who might you be, young fella?"

"Ade," said Ade. "My name is A-Dee Not Eddie, not Adrian, and definitely not

Ade, like at the end of lemonade."

"Oh, he's sharp, isn't he?" Glenn said. "You got a right one there, love."

But Ade's mum wasn't listening any more. Her eye had been drawn to something on the stall.

"How about that one?" she said, pointing. "How much would that be?"

Ade followed his mum's finger to where she was pointing. There, blazing out amongst the nice, normal black, grey and dark blue suits, was the brightest pink checked blazer with matching flared trousers that Ade, or indeed anyone, had ever seen.

"Well, well, well, Mrs Apepijan!" said Glenn.

"ADEPITAN," she corrected him.

"Pardon me, madam," said the stallholder. "Now then, you certainly know your fashion, don't you? This is a lovely number. Hundred per cent wool, guaranteed not to shrink."

As Glenn started to go into his sales patter, Ade felt his heart sink. *No, surely not,* he thought. *Mum can't be thinking about buying that suit for me.* It was louder and brighter than the Big Bang.

"Oh yeah," Glenn continued. "You're definitely gonna make an impression in this suit. No one's gonna miss you, that's for sure. It's a great colour. What's the occasion? Party? Wedding? Carnival?"

"Oh no," said Ade's mum. "It's for Ade to wear tomorrow; it's his first day of school."

Glenn paused. He gulped. He looked at Ade with pity.

"First day of school?" he said. "Well, it's very nice and that, but don't you think it'd be better for him to try something a little less, erm, colourful?"

A wide-eyed Ade nodded furiously.

"Yes, Mum." He pointed at a very plain black suit. "That one might be bett–"

"Oh no." Mum cut him off. "This is most definitely the one. It's beautiful." Then, to confirm her belief, she picked up the blazer and added, "Yes and very good quality material, as well."

Glenn looked at Ade and then shrugged as if to say, *Sorry, mate. A sale is a sale.*

That's it, I'm done for. Ade knew there was no escape. *Mum's going to buy me not only the worst suit in London, not even the worst suit in the UK, but also the worst suit in the entire world.*

Ade bit his lip. Not even the Parsons Road Gang would want to hang out with the boy with the funny walk and the pink, checked, flared suit. *I'm going to be a giant, limping stick of candyfloss.*

Ade blinked hard. He was back in his room, memories of yesterday swiftly fading.

"Go get your suit, then." Mum was sitting on the edge of the bed.

Slowly, Ade dragged himself out of bed and went over to the cupboard. "Please have changed colour in the night," he whispered to himself.

He opened the door. The suit hadn't changed colour. If anything it beamed out at him even more brightly than yesterday. Full-on pinky checked-ness.

Ade gritted his teeth. The suit wasn't going anywhere. It was time to get this over and done with. He chuckled to himself. *If I don't laugh, I'll cry*. He just hoped that he'd still be laughing at the end of the day.

CHAPTER 13

FASHION SHOW!

"So handsome!" said Ade's mum as he headed towards the front door.

He caught a glimpse of himself in the hallway mirror. To complete his 'look', Ade's mum had combed his hair into a massive Afro, which made his head look like a giant microphone. And, to finish things off, she'd made him wear a large, black velvet bow tie!

I look ridiculous.

"My boy! You look amazing." Dad was beaming.

They're so proud, Ade thought. *Their son. Their son who had polio and wears a caliper on his leg is going to a regular school like all the other kids.*

Ade knew it hadn't been easy. Mr Thomas, the head teacher at Credon Road Primary, had expressed serious reservations. The school was nearly a hundred years old, parts of it had been bombed during the Second World War and the building had been reconstructed on three floors. Getting around involved climbing up and down stairs, lots of stairs.

Ade knew that he would be the first disabled child of any kind to attend the school. And it was happening because his parents had both dreamed and fought so hard for this moment.

They are full of pride and I'm just full of fear, Ade realised. *Fear about what people will laugh at first, my leg, my dodgy suit or my crazy hair. Perhaps they'll end up so confused they'll just leave me alone.*

As Ade stepped out of the front door he was beginning to think that his mother wasn't completely deluded. Maybe she was actually a genius. What if she had made her son look as geeky as possible on purpose? What if she'd done it so the bullies wouldn't know where to start with him?

Ade shook his head in frustration. *Or the bullies all queue up to get me on my first day?*

Ade turned and looked back at his parents, who were standing together by the front door and waving. "Remember," Mum called. "No football with your new caliper."

Ade nodded and managed to make it to the garden gate without anyone on the street giving him any grief which, under the circumstances, was quite an achievement. He smiled weakly back at his mum and dad, and walked on.

Dexter, Brian and Shed all came out of their houses at the same time. As they reached their front gates, they all looked at Ade standing on the pavement.

Dexter was the first to speak. "All right, Ade," he said in an unusually shy voice.

Dexter was wearing a bright red jumper and a pair of black trousers with red pinstripes running down them. Over that he had a huge parka coat that was about two sizes too big for him.

Ade covered his mouth, trying not to laugh.

"What!?" Dexter shouted defiantly. "It's my brother's coat. I'll grow into it! Anyway, what are you wearing? MISTER PINK SUIT."

Dexter said the last bit in a posh, high-pitched voice, which made them both start giggling.

"Oi, what are you two laughing at?" said Brian, standing in his gateway. He was wearing a pair of brown corduroy trousers and a yellow tank top over a white shirt, a combination that only made Ade and Dexter laugh even harder. Brian couldn't see the funny side. He thought he looked smart. He'd picked out the tank top personally.

Finally, they all turned and looked at Shed as he walked towards them wearing an ill-fitting pair of lime green jeans. They were at least two sizes too small for him and made him look like a young version of the Incredible Hulk. He also had on a smart shirt with his sleeves rolled up to the elbow.

The four of them really were quite a sight, a sort of weird rainbow of clothes, and soon they were all falling about laughing.

"Seriously, I think we all look cool," Brian said, trying his best to keep a straight face.

"Looks like your mums have all been getting fashion tips from mine," Ade replied.

Suddenly, a shrill voice came from the upstairs window of Dexter's house. "Oi, Dexter, stop jabbering and get to school. If you don't hurry up you'll be late."

It was Dexter's mum. She still had curlers in her hair and her face was bright red. This would usually have made the boys laugh even more, but she sounded quite cross, so they all tried hard to look as serious as possible and started walking to school. Once they were out of sight, and sure Dexter's mum couldn't hear them, they all cracked up and started making fun of each other's clothes again.

Maybe the other kids at school would see the funny side of it as well and they'd all end up having a big laugh about it.

Maybe.

CHAPTER 14

PLAYGROUND PANIC

Ade leant back and craned his neck upwards. Credon Road Primary School was three storeys high. Huge arched windows lined up in rows on each floor and in combination with the dark brown bricks that surrounded them, the school looked quite sinister against the grey cloudy sky.

Apart from the hospital, this was going to be the tallest building he'd ever been in and, unlike the hospital, there were no lifts, broken or unbroken, if he needed them. Looking up at the top row of windows, he imagined climbing all the stairs and gulped.

Turning his attention back to ground level, Ade looked at his friends. They all seemed as nervous as he was, but it wasn't the building they were concerned about.

Walking into the playground, Ade and his friends were confronted by a teeming mass of children running, skipping, chasing, jumping and, in some cases, just standing around chatting. The noise was incredible; you could probably hear it from at least two streets away.

"I'd forgotten how big this place was," Dexter said.

"And noisy," Brian added. "I can hardly hear myself think."

"It's not Southern Road Playing Fields, that's for sure." Shed sounded wistful.

This whole time I didn't want to go to school, Ade thought. *I didn't really think about how the rest of them were feeling.* They'd had the best summer together and now it was all going to change. *It was just the four of us and now there are hundreds of kids to deal with.*

"Hey," Ade said as cheerily as possible.

"What?" they all replied.

"Never forget, we're the Parsons Road Gang!"

Brian smiled. Dexter nodded, and Shed looked at the boys and said proudly, "Yeah, and we always stick together!"

"Yeah!" shouted the other three, punching the air.

DOOFF!

A leather football hit Brian square on the nose. Ade watched as his friend's blue-rimmed glasses flew off his face.

Brian wiped his nose, realised there was no blood then dropped to his knees and instantly began scrabbling around on the playground trying to find his glasses. Shed and Dexter helped.

Ade spotted the glasses next to a water fountain and picked them up, but saw straight away that the left lens had shattered, creating a pattern that looked like a spider's web in the glass.

"You all right, Brian?" said Ade, passing them back to his friend. "Afraid they're a bit broken."

"My mum's going to kill me," said Brian, gingerly putting them back on. "But at least they're not completely broken, even if it does feel like I'm looking out of a kaleidoscope."

"Oi! Give our ball back, you freaks!" said an unpleasant-sounding voice.

Standing there with three other kids was a short, but extremely stocky, boy with dark curly hair, pale skin and round, puffy cheeks.

"Oh no!" muttered Dexter. "Spencer Frogley."

"We don't know where your ball is," Shed said. Even though Shed was pretty big, his voice sounded rather small.

"But when you find it, be careful where you kick it from now on," Ade added. "You broke Brian's glasses."

As Ade spoke, he noticed that Spencer's eyes seemed to bulge out of his head and double in size, making him *actually* look like a frog. A frog with curly hair.

"Are you telling me what to do?" Spencer looked round at his cronies like he couldn't quite believe it. "Look at the state of you all."

“What a bunch of muppets,” said one of Spencer’s friends. “They must have escaped from the circus.”

As the boys laughed, Ade could feel every child in the playground staring at him and his friends. Ade’s stomach began to churn as he felt a mixture of anger and fear. It was the same sort of feeling he’d had in Queen's Market the first time he'd been there. And when he'd seen Deano and Sam outside his house on the day of the party.

Ade looked at his friends. Shed was looking down intently at something on the ground, while Brian was busy trying to adjust his broken glasses.

"I think the frame is twisted," he muttered anxiously under his breath.

Even Dexter was unusually quiet.

"Come on, freaks, the ball's right next to you," shouted Spencer. "Don't you know how to use your arms? Chuck the ball back!"

Ade glared at Spencer and then, without thinking, he picked up the football and with an almighty heave of his right arm, threw it as hard as he could towards the other boys, who were still laughing amongst themselves.

The ball sailed over their heads and through the goal Spencer and his friends had made using their coats.

"**GOOOAAAL!**" Ade screamed in the style of a Brazilian commentator.

Shed suddenly looked up and beamed at Ade.

"Yeah, Cyborg Cat does it again!" shouted Dexter, springing to life and laughing hysterically.

"Take it easy, guys," Brian hissed. He glanced in the direction of Spencer and his mates. "They're coming over."

"You think that was funny?" Spencer said angrily once he was practically face-to-face with Ade.

"If you mean the fact that I managed to throw a football into your goal without hitting your huge head then, yes," Ade replied with a smirk.

Spencer's friends started to giggle, but stopped suddenly when he turned and glared at them.

"Look, gentlemen, there seems to have been a slight misunderstanding," Brian started to say, using what he called his calming voice; the one he used whenever the boys needed something from grown-ups. "Why don't we all– "

"Shut it, Four Eyes," Spencer growled. He turned back to Ade.

They glared at each other. **It. Was. On.**

CHAPTER 15

PLAY THAT MELODY

Ade knew for a fact that he wasn't going to blink first. He was really good at this game. He used to play it with his cousin at Gran-gran's house.

"Erm, I've got an idea," Dexter said. "And it doesn't involve eyeballing each other."

One of Spencer's mates lunged towards him, but Spencer blocked him with an arm. "Let's hear what the idiot in the red jumper's got to say."

Dexter took a deep breath. "Why don't we sort this out with a football match? Your team against us lot, the Parsons Road Gang."

Spencer looked at Dexter and started laughing again. "The what gang?" he said.

This time, Spencer's friends and a large group of children who had gathered round to see what was going on all broke into fits of laughter.

"You bunch of freaks don't stand a chance!" Spencer said, high-fiving his friends. "We're the best players in this school." He pointed at two of his friends. One of them was skinny with blonde hair and freckles. The other boy was dark-haired with huge, powerful legs that looked like tree trunks. "Stuart and John go to West Ham's junior academy," Spencer said with a swagger. "We'd run rings round you."

"So, you're saying you won't take us on?" said Dexter.

"What do you think, lads?" said Spencer to John and Stuart.

The academy stars shrugged. "Yeah, why not?" said John. "It'll kill time before school starts."

"Right," said Spencer, pointing to the goal Ade had just thrown the ball through. "See you for your total annihilation. Over there, in two minutes."

Spencer and his friends walked off to prepare for the match.

Ade's shoulders drooped and he breathed for what felt like the first time in ages. Then he turned to Dexter.

"You idiot." His voice was trembling.

"What you worried about, Ade?" said Dexter, putting a calming hand on Ade's shoulder. "This will be easy."

"Yeah, we can take them," agreed Shed. "We've been practising all summer; we're more than ready for this challenge."

Ade looked at the boys and shook his head. "Haven't you all forgotten something?" he said.

The boys looked at Ade, bemused. "What?" they said as one.

"No more football. I can't play. My mum said I'm not supposed to in case my caliper breaks!"

Ade's words hit the boys like a ton of bricks. Dexter went pale, Shed swallowed hard and said in shock, "**No Cyborg Cat?**" Brian let out a huge sigh and started to fiddle nervously with his smashed glasses.

"What's the matter, you freaks, chickening out?" Spencer jeered.

"Th... there see... see... seems to be a slight problem," Brian stuttered. "A crucial member of our team," Brian paused and nodded in Ade's direction, "can't play because his Mu... erm, no, because he's injured."

Spencer focused his bulgy eyes on Ade. "You mean he can't play because he's a stupid peg leg cripple!"

More laughter broke out. There were some gasps and squeals as some of the children nearby noticed Ade's leg and, in particular his hospital boots and the iron rods coming out of the heel. Ade felt sick. It felt like everyone was staring at him.

"Look," said Dexter amidst the commotion. "How about we make it three against three?"

"No way," spat Spencer. "*You* challenged us to this match; if you haven't got enough players on your side that's not our problem."

"But that's not fair!" shouted Shed.

"Yeah," chipped in Brian. "And I can only see out of one eye 'cause you broke my glasses."

"Shouldn't have got your stupid big nose in the way of the ball then, should you?" retorted Spencer. "Now, we gonna start or what?"

"I'll play on their team."

The voice came from somewhere amongst the kids who had gathered around the two rival groups.

A tall girl with springy black hair forced her way to the front of the crowd. She looked familiar and Ade realised it was the girl from the bus stop. The boys all stood in silence and stared, open-mouthed. She walked over to Ade and his team.

"I'm Melody Roberts," she said. "I'm in the same year as you."

Ade and his friends looked at each

other, then back at Melody. They seemed unable to speak.

Melody shook her head, clearly unimpressed, and said, "Are you boys gonna stand there like total idiots or are we going to beat those other idiots over there?"

Ade and the gang continued to look at each other. Ade knew what was befuddling their brains because it was befuddling his brain, too.

"She's a girl," Shed eventually blurted out.

"She's a girl," Melody responded, mimicking Shed's voice. "Wow, we've got a smart one here."

"This is just perfect," yelled Spencer. "They've swapped the cripple for a girl!"

Melody glowered fiercely in Spencer's direction then grabbed the football and began doing keepy-uppies.

When she got to 20, Ade's brain clicked back in to gear. He'd suddenly realised two things. They had to win this game or end up being the butt of the whole school's jokes for the rest of their time at Credon, and they had to have Melody on their team.

"**LET'S START,**" he shouted. "If I can't play, I'll be the manager. Brian, you go in goal; Dexter, up front with Melody."

"Hey, Melody," said Dexter. "I'm just warning you now to cover your eyes, as you're about to be dazzled by the best right foot in London."

"We'll see about that," said Melody as the two of them raced off, passing the ball between them as they went.

"What about me, gaffer?" said Shed, looking at Ade.

"Midfield, of course, Shed. Make sure nothing gets past you."

Shed pounded his chest and gave Ade a determined look. Moments later, it was kick-off.

CHAPTER 16

THE MOST IMPORTANT MATCH OF THEIR LIVES

Ade stood on the sidelines, pacing up and down. The first few exchanges were fast and furious. It was clear that Stuart and John were pretty good, but Shed was doing his job in midfield and, with Dexter and Melody tracking back and helping him out, the two academy trainees weren't able to break through.

Brian was also doing well in goal, despite only really being able to see out of one eye, and, after he'd saved a shot from Spencer, he spotted Melody free on the right and threw the ball out to her.

Melody trapped it and immediately set off. *Her close control is fantastic*, Ade thought as he watched her dribble round all of Spencer's team. She approached the goal and Ade held his breath as she skillfully slotted the ball past Spencer's goalkeeper.

"**GOOOAL!**" yelled Ade, whooping in delight. "What an unbelievable goal!"

Melody high-fived Dexter and just laughed at Shed, who was still speechless and in awe of their new star player.

"Come on." Spencer was furious. "We're not getting beaten by this bunch of weirdos!"

By now, pretty much the whole school had gathered round to watch the match.

Even the teacher on morning playground duty was watching intently from a distance.

Ade could see that Spencer's rage, and the fact that they'd gone a goal down, seemed to energise his team. *They're getting it together*, he thought, watching a slick passing move between John and Stuart. Then in a flash it happened – an incisive pass from John put Stuart through on goal. Ade knew what was coming. Stuart blasted the ball towards the left-hand corner of the goal.

Brian looked to have it covered, but as he was about to dive towards the ball, he lost his footing and hit the ground. Once again, his glasses flew off his face.

"**YESSS!**" cheered Stuart, punching the air with a clenched fist as the ball flew into the goal to make the score 1-1.

"That's more like it, lads," Spencer screamed, his eyes bulging so much they almost came out of their sockets. He gave Stuart a bear hug and lifted him off the ground in celebration.

"Looks like luck's running out for the Pampers Road Gang!" Spencer yelled, pointing at Ade.

Ade raced over to Brian, flicked the lever on his caliper and knelt down beside him. His friend was looking slightly dazed with his broken glasses in his hands.

"Are you okay?" Ade asked as Shed, Dexter and Melody came over.

Brian got to his feet, swayed on the spot and took a step towards the wall. "I feel a bit funny," he said. "Don't think I can play any more." He held up what was left of his glasses. "These have had it."

"Er, Brian," Ade started to say, but before he could finish, Brian raised his hand to interrupt.

In his best calming voice, he said, "Ade, I know your mum said you're not allowed to play football but, listen to me, we need you. The Parsons Road Gang needs you!"

"I will listen to you, Brian," said Ade. "But first you need to turn around, because you're talking to a wall. I'm behind you."

"Ah!" Brian turned round. "I hit my head harder than I thought."

"Come on, Pampers Gang! We haven't got all day." Spencer's voice was loud and mocking.

Ade looked at Spencer. *If we don't win this game, all the other kids in the school will treat me and my friends the way Spencer is treating us now.* He also knew that his parents would kill him if he played football and something happened to his caliper.

"Come on, Cripple Boy," Spencer taunted. "What are you lot doing?"

Cripple. Ade hated that word. It was what that horrible man in Queen's Market had called him. *It does not describe me.*

"I'll go in goal," Ade said.

"Yes!" Dexter exclaimed. "Get ready for Cyborg Cat."

Ade took up his position. He knew this could all end very badly. *What if the teachers tell my parents I played football? Or my caliper breaks again?* But he didn't really have a choice. He wasn't going to let his friends down and he needed to show everyone what he was capable of.

The game restarted. Spencer's team launched wave after wave of attack, but the Parsons Road defence held firm. When

a shot did get through, Ade was ready. Cyborg Cat made three spectacular saves and then Shed somehow managed to get the ball off one of the other players. Ade smiled to himself when he saw that Spencer was getting angrier and angrier.

From the sidelines, Brian, who was holding the one good lens from his glasses to his right eye, hollered, "Through ball, Shed."

Shed was not known for his accuracy when it came to passing but, to Brian and everyone else's surprise, he coolly lofted the perfect pass over Spencer to Melody.

Melody controlled the ball with one touch and looked up. Dexter was up front screaming, "I'm open. Get it to my right foot!"

A moment later, Melody had crossed the ball beautifully to Dexter. As it came over he pulled his right foot back, ready to hit the ball sweetly and bury it in the back of the net, even though there was no net. It would probably have been one of the greatest goals ever scored in Credon Primary School playground had it not been for the fact that Dexter missed the ball completely.

Ade groaned, but then the ball ricocheted off Dexter's right foot, bounced up and struck him in the face. The goalie had already flung himself towards the shot he was expecting, and Spencer and his team could only watch in horror as the ball rolled across the line, making it 2-1 to the Parsons Road Gang.

Ade, Shed, Brian and Melody jumped in the air, screaming with delight.

"Did I score?" said Dexter, rubbing his nose.

"Of course you did, you sausage," Brian bellowed, and the whole team huddled together and began to jump on the spot.

"It's not over yet!" Spencer hollered. He picked up the ball and restarted the game while the Parsons Road Gang and Melody were still celebrating.

"Oi," yelled Ade, trying to get back to his goal.

"Yeah, wait a minute," shouted Dexter.

But it was too late. Spencer had passed the ball to Stuart, who took a shot at the empty goal.

CHAPTER 17

CYBORG CAT

Shed launched himself through the air and made a last-ditch crunching tackle. He didn't connect with the ball, but he did connect with Stuart's legs, sending him to the ground in a painful heap.

"Penalty!" yelled Spencer. "That's got to be a penalty."

Ade nodded. *Yeah, that's fair.* Even though the Parson's Road Gang hadn't been ready to restart the game, he had to admit, it was a terrible tackle.

Shed ran over to Stuart who was writhing on the ground clutching his ankle. "Sorry, mate," he said.

"No worries." Stuart jumped to his feet with a grin. "We've got a penalty."

"I'm taking it." Spencer picked up the ball and walked over to Ade's goal. He then counted out 10 paces and put the ball down. "This is the penalty spot," he announced.

Ade thought it seemed a bit too close to the goal, but no one else questioned it.

"You can do it, Ade," shouted Shed from the sidelines. "Cyborg Cat's got this."

"Yeah," shouted the others.

THUDDD! Spencer hammered the ball as hard as he could towards the goal.

As it hurtled through the air, Ade imagined he really was Cyborg Cat. *I'm as fast as a cat and strong as a cyborg.* He launched himself to his right, with his arm stretched out as far as it would go.

CRACK!

The ball hit Ade's outstretched fingertips. It was just enough to push it wide of the goal by a centimetre.

DUMPH! Ade hit the concrete playground floor. Not even the shoulder pads in his pink suit could protect him from the painful landing.

There was silence. Then the teacher's whistle. Class was about to start. The match was over.

Dexter, Shed, Brian and Melody came running over. Ade had sat up but wasn't ready to stand.

"Yesss!" screamed Dexter. "The Super Cyborg Cat Adepitan saves the day."

"I told you we could do it," Shed shouted.

"That's 2-1 to the Parsons Road Gang!" Brian hollered.

Melody leapt in the air singing, "Championes, championes, *ole ole ole*!"

Ade could see that the whole playground had erupted into celebration.

"Nice work, new boy," one of the older pupils yelled over to him. Another gave him a thumbs up.

Maybe school wasn't going to be too bad, after all, Ade thought.

John and Stuart came over. "Good game, guys."

Ade noticed that Spencer was nowhere to be seen. *He's gone off to sulk*.

As the crowd dispersed and poured into school, Ade began to dust himself off. Pink did not look good dirty! He froze. "Uh-oh."

"What's wrong?" said Shed.

Ade looked towards his leg, "I think I've broken it."

"No!" shouted Brian with a look of dread on his face.

Ade looked at the gang solemnly. "Yeah. I think I've broken a toenail on my left foot."

It took a moment for the gang to realise what he'd said. Then they all burst out laughing.

"You silly sausage!" Brian shouted and with that, the boys all piled on top of Ade and continued celebrating.

Melody stood and watched, shaking her head and smiling. "You lot are ridiculous," she said as the teacher blew the whistle again for final warning to get to class.

For the rest of the school day the Parsons Road Gang and Melody were heroes. Everyone had seen the morning's

events. Ade even heard someone call them 'The Spencer Slayers!'

Dexter suggested putting this on T-shirts and selling them.

"Not so sure about that," Ade had responded. He had a feeling Spencer was going to be someone they needed to avoid and rubbing his face it in would definitely not be a good idea.

At the end of school, the boys waved goodbye to Melody as she jumped on her blue Raleigh BMX with white mag wheels.

"She's amazing!" Shed said. "Even her bike is supercool."

"Yes, she's quite remarkable," said Brian. "For a girl."

"She's quite remarkable for a human being," said Ade. "She's got to be the best footballer I've ever seen."

Brian and Shed nodded their heads in agreement.

Dexter shrugged. "She needs to work on her left foot."

Ade grinned. "She's not the only one."

They walked on towards Parsons Road.

"So, still think school is going to be horrible, Ade?" Shed asked.

Ade grinned. "Nah, today's been great. Better than great, actually. I don't think it could get any bett..."

He trailed off as he heard the rhythmic sound of a ball bouncing on concrete, followed by another noise, one he'd never heard before.

"What *is* that?" Brian said.

A moment later, Brian's question was answered when an LA Lakers basketball suddenly appeared in front of them. It bounced on the pavement and then, before it could bounce again, a long, powerful arm reached out and grabbed it.

It was quite a move. Ade watched as an athletic-looking young boy sped up alongside them. He wasn't running, though. He was in a bright red wheelchair with white discs in the middle of the wheels. Each disc had been painted with red, yellow and orange flames, which made it look like the wheels were on fire as they whizzed round. The unusual noise Ade and his friends had heard was the wheelchair's tyres making a skidding sound as the boy used his hands to control it.

"**WHOA!**" Ade, Dexter, Shed and Brian said in unison.

"All right," said the boy in the chair as he briskly rolled past, skilfully controlling the basketball and his wheelchair at the same time.

He didn't look much older than Ade and his friends, but his muscular physique and powerful arms made him look twice their size. He was wearing a basketball vest with the words 'Newham Rollers' on the front.

"Who was that?" asked Ade as the boy zoomed off and became a dot in the distance.

Shed shook his head. "I don't know, but I think that was the coolest thing I've ever seen."

"Yeah, I suppose so," Ade muttered under his breath.

For some reason he felt a bit weird. He'd always thought using a wheelchair meant that a person was helpless. But that boy wasn't helpless. He wasn't being pushed. He was moving himself. And the wheelchair wasn't slowing him down. It was speeding him up.

It would be amazing to move that fast, Ade thought. *But isn't walking always supposed to be better?* He felt confused and guilty thinking this stuff. It made him want to change the subject, and change it quickly.

"Come on, let's get home and practise a few shots before dinner time," Ade said. "Spencer might want a rematch."

Dexter put a hand out. Ade, Shed and Brian did the same, and they all performed the Parsons Road Gang handshake.

"Spencer can do what he likes," Brian said. "Because, together, we're invincible."

"Yes, we are!" the Parsons Road Gang said as one.

Look out for more adventures
from me – the Cyborg Cat and
the Parsons Road Gang.